HELPERS

First published 1975 by The Bodley Head
First published in Picture Lions 1978
by William Collins Sons & Co Ltd
8 Grafton Street, London W1X 3LA

© Shirley Hughes 1975

Printed in Great Britain
by William Collins Sons & Co Ltd, Glasgow

HELPERS

Shirley Hughes

FONTANA
PICTURE LIONS

Mick, Jenny and Baby Sue's
mother has to go out today
and leave them behind.

George has come to look after
them. He is nearly grown-up,
and a very good helper.

"Now," says George, "there's
going to be no mucking about.
You've all got to help."

They clear the dirty things from the
table and stack them on the sink.
Not one is broken.

Sue doesn't help. She sits in her
high chair, dropping bits of
crust on the floor.

"Looks a bit of a mess in here,"
says George in the children's room.
"The beds aren't very well made . . .

there are comics all over the floor . . .

and who's been walking about in
muddy wellingtons?"

The toy cupboard looks like this.
It's too full to put anything away.

George says that there would be a lot more room if they threw away some of these old broken toys.

BAH!

Mick is a great help in carrying them out to the bin.

But Jenny thinks

it rather a pity

to get rid of

so many old friends.

Luckily Sue has cleared an entire
shelf of the bookcase all by herself.

It's just right as a home for old toys.

Now it is
time for Sue to
go into her pram

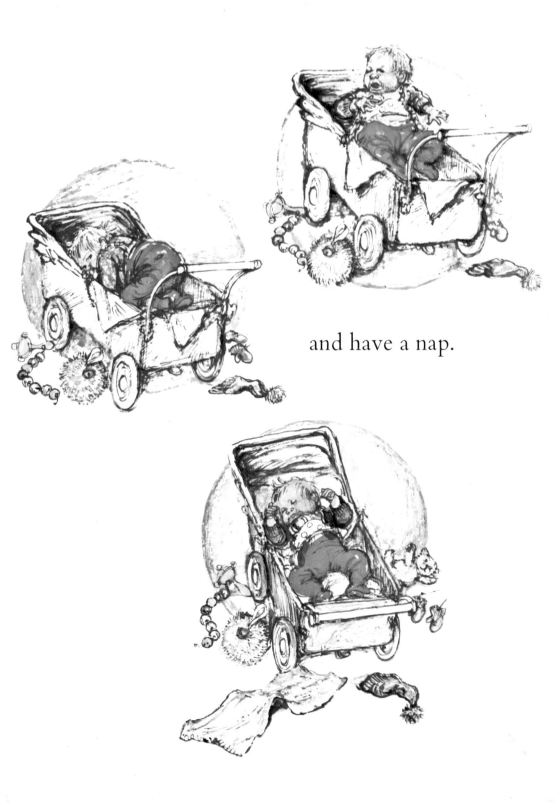

and have a nap.

The others go into the garden. It's much too small for football, but there are four flowers out.

"Perhaps we could do some weeding," says George.

But Mick and Jenny aren't quite sure which are the weeds and which are the plants. Neither is George, so they pick the flowers instead to make a lovely bunch for Mum when she comes in.

Suddenly everyone's hungry!
Mum has left a cold dinner—
Hooray! Jenny thinks she can
remember how the knives, forks and
spoons go. Right hand? Left hand?
  Has she done it properly?
  Mick helps Sue with her
chocolate pudding.

After dinner George sits down to
read his magazine. The children
play a game of boats with cushions.
The shiny part of the floor is the sea
and the carpet is the land.

Sue keeps getting out of her boat into the water. When there is a shipwreck they have to climb up George to keep from being drowned.

George soon says crossly that he's had enough of this game, so they go out to the shop.

At the shop George buys some chewing gum for himself and some sweets for the children.

Sue sits outside in her pram,
chatting to friends.

On the way home they call at
the "rec". George pushes
everyone *very* high on the swings.

When they get home George thinks he will finish off painting the sitting-room window frame.

But this is not a good idea.

They all watch television instead.

Suddenly George remembers
that none of the washing up
has been done.

Now Mick and Jenny do a really
helpful thing. They give Sue a bath
all by themselves. They make
sure that the water isn't too hot, and
hold on tight while they soap her
all over. Afterwards they put on her
nightie and even remember to
brush her hair.

There's someone at the door.
Mum's come home!

Now it's time for the children to
have their supper and go to bed.
Mum says they've all been very
good.

How could George have managed
without them?